The Story of the Search for the Story

written by
Bjørn Sortland

illustrated by
Lars Elling

CAROLRHODA BOOKS, INC./MINNEAPOLIS

Once upon a time, there was a boy named Henry who was very fond of books. Each evening, his uncle would read him a story.

That's how this story should begin—and that's how it did begin, two sentences ago. But it was really Henry who read to Uncle Richard, because Uncle Richard was afraid he'd get his library books wet in the bathtub.

"What are you going to read to us tonight, my young bookworm?" Uncle Richard asked. Henry shut his eyes, as usual, and pulled a book from the shelf. It was called *The Story of the Search for the Story.* Oddly enough, there was no author's name on the cover and the pages were blank. When Henry flipped through the book, letters fell out helter-skelter.

"Look, Uncle, this book is just empty pages and a few loose letters," said Henry.

Uncle Richard took the book from Henry and inspected it carefully. "Well, well, this is not good. You must see if you can find another copy of this book, one that has more in it. You know where the library is, don't you?"

"Um, sort of. I'll find it all right," Henry said.

But Henry wasn't really sure where the library was. He went out his uncle's front door and down the gravel drive—past all the mailboxes, past the unpainted house, across the lawn that's never been mown—to a narrow path that was a shortcut to the park.

"There, on the other side of the park," thought Henry. "That's where the library must be."

It was autumn, the time of year Henry liked best, when the trees glow with color and the clear air makes it seem like anything can happen. A strong wind was blowing all sorts of things around.

Henry caught sight of a paper airplane sailing through the air. He leaped up and caught it. There was a message written on it:

HELP! Authors seek a main character. We need a brave young man in a stylish cap.

S. B. and others

"Strange," thought Henry, looking around. Should he be reading something between the lines here? There were no authors in sight. But lying on a bench was a green cap. Henry put it on. It was a bit too big and fell down over his eyes. When Henry pushed the cap off his face, he suddenly discovered . . .

. . . that somehow everything seemed to have changed. Also, suddenly, two men stood before him.

"Nice cap," said the man with the glasses. "You're made for it."

"Do you know where the library is?" asked Henry. "I—I'm looking for a book—a story."

The man in the yellow suit leaned across to Henry and whispered, "A story, you say. Listen to your thoughts and dreams and you'll hear all sorts of stories."

"Who are you, and where am I?" asked Henry, confused.

"I'm Knut Hamsun," said the man in the yellow suit.

"I'm James Joyce," said the man with the glasses. "And where are you? Well, Dublin might be a good place to begin a tale. Dublin on the sixteenth of June, nineteen hundred and four."

"But I'm really looking for a book," Henry explained again. "I think it's in the library. Do either of you know where the library is?"

"Better go to the sea," said Hamsun. "Its savage wildness has inspired many a story."

"And where's the sea from here?" Henry asked.

The two men looked at each other and shrugged.

"Hey," piped a clear, high-pitched voice. "If it's the sea you're looking for, I know where it is."

In the distance, Henry spied a girl with two red braids. There was something familiar about her.

"You can find the sea on the very next page," laughed the girl.

And she was right! A soft summer breeze caressed Henry's face.

"Excuse me," said Henry to an Englishwoman holding on to her hat. "Do you know if there's a library here? I'm looking for a book."

"What kind of book?" asked Virginia Woolf.

"I'm not sure," said Henry. "My uncle wants it. It's some sort of story."

"Perhaps it is a story about everything that streams through our thoughts, like a lemon yellow sailing boat, a color that's bluer than blue, the sound of clocks striking, a lighthouse, and this beautiful horizon, which will still be here in a million years, after we are all gone . . . ."

"You sound like an author," Henry said. "Was it you who sent that paper airplane in search of a main character?"

"No, that's not how I find my characters. But now that you mention it, I do need a young boy for the book I'm about to write."

"I really should keep looking for the library," said Henry. "Do you know where it is?"

"I'm afraid there's no library nearby. But I can send you across the sea to an American I know of. He brags a lot, but he's sure to help you with a story."

Before Henry could say another word, the woman took out a pen and wrote in her notebook:

The boy with the stylish cap was suddenly sent across the sea to . . .

. . . a room where a powerful looking man was sitting behind a desk.

"And where are you from?" asked the man, whose name was Ernest Hemingway.

"From the other side of the sea," said Henry, not quite sure if he believed it himself. "Are you a librarian?"

Hemingway laughed. "No. But I work with books. Right now, I'm writing a story about a boy who lives by the sea and old Santiago, his friend. I think it might be one of my better stories."

"I see," said Henry. "I'm actually searching for another story—"

"The old man's luck has deserted him," interrupted Hemingway, "so he can no longer catch a single fish . . ."

And so Henry listened to the story. The old man at long last catches the biggest fish he's ever hooked. It's so big that Santiago has to tow it home behind his boat. On the way, sharks eat more and more of the huge fish, until there is nothing left but bones.

"I think that's how it must go," said Hemingway. "And if I know that old man, he got tired and lay down to sleep and dreamed of lions."

"You're a good storyteller, but I have to find the library," said Henry. "I have to find my own story, you see."

"First you must meet the lady who's visiting me," Hemingway said. "Many know her as Isak Dinesen. She's a living library."

Henry looked into the next room and saw a small, thin woman sitting in a large chair and gazing dreamily into the fire.

"Hi," said Henry. "I'm searching for the library and a story, but I keep getting lost."

"That doesn't matter—I've got masses of stories in here," said the woman, tapping her forehead with a bony finger. "If you just let your imagination go, it's easy to find the most fantastic stories. Give me a sentence, or just a word, and we'll see."

"But I—" said Henry, "I—"

"I. Yes," said the woman. "That's a word often used in literature. I . . . let me see, I was . . . no. I had a farm, a farm in Africa . . ."

Time melted away. Henry sat staring into the fire and heard of foreign markets where silk and scimitars are sold, of scorching sun and months of rain, of safaris and lion hunts deep in the African savanna. Just as day dawned and the lions were padding out to drink at the watering hole, Henry heard an engine in the distance.

"Perhaps that's my dear friend Denys Finch-Hatton, the great hunter, arriving in his airplane," said the woman dreamily. "Go with him and you may find what you're looking for."

"You're not the Little Prince," said the pilot, who had helped Henry aboard his plane. He looked disappointed.

"No, I'm Henry. Are you the great hunter Denys Finch-Hatton?" asked Henry as the plane took off.

"No, that's not me. I'm Antoine de Saint-Exupéry. For a moment, I thought you were the Little Prince from Asteroid B-612. I met him once when I had to make an emergency landing in the desert. I haven't given up believing and hoping I'll see him again. Somehow I feel he's always close by."

"What's he like?" asked Henry.

"He's extremely wise and handsome," said the pilot. The first thing he did was ask me to draw a sheep for him."

"And did you?" Henry asked.

"Yes, I did, even though it seemed far more important to repair my plane. But the Little Prince taught me that it's not our eyes that see the important things, but our hearts. What about you—what's important to you?"

Henry told the pilot about the book with the blank pages, the paper airplane, the green cap, all the people he'd met, and the library he couldn't seem to find.

"It's a great story," said the pilot." And now that you mention it, I've seen a lot of paper airplanes lately. When we land in Paris, you must go to 102 Boulevard Haussmann. There's someone there who may be able to help you."

At 102 Boulevard Haussmann, Henry's eyes took a long time to adjust to the darkness. Inside, it seemed like neither day nor night. Could this be the library?

"Excuse me, I'm searching for a book," he said. "Are you the librarian?"

"No, I'm the author—Marcel Proust," sighed a man with tassels on his slippers. "But today I can't write anything. All my cakes, my madeleines, have vanished. How am I to write when I'm missing my dear little madeleines?"

"Cakes?" said Henry. "You need cakes to write?"

"We writers often need strange things to achieve what we want. And just at this moment, I need madeleines."

"Why?" Henry asked.

Proust began to cough. "I ate them when I was young. Now they help me to hold on to time for a brief moment, to remember what it was like to be your age, for example."

Henry was about to ask about the way to the library, when all of a sudden he caught sight of someone through the big window. Could it be? . . .

"Thanks for the chat," said Henry quickly. "Maybe we could talk another time."

"I doubt that very much," said the man, and he started to cough again.

Henry hurried out to the street. There she was, complete with carrot-red hair and freckles, and she was eating something that looked very much like a madeleine.

"I didn't do it. It was my monkey, Mr. Nilsson. He crept in through the window and stole the cakes. I'm only eating them." The girl gave Henry an innocent look. "But I did ask him to leave a gold coin."

"I thought you might have had something to do with it," said Henry, who was feeling a bit shy. "I've read about you. You're Pippi Longstocking."

"I know who you are, too," said Pippi. "You're the main character in this story. You're probably looking for a happy ending, like I am. I'm searching for my parents. My mother's an angel in heaven, so she may be hard to find. But Papa should be easier. He's a cannibal king on the island of Kurrekurredutt. What are you searching for?"

"I'm looking for the library," Henry explained. "I have to find a book for my uncle."

"Why didn't you say so right away, at the beginning of the story?" Pippi exclaimed. "I was in the park, you know. Didn't you see me?"

"You told me how to get to the sea!" said Henry. "I thought that was you!"

"Climb up onto my horse," said Pippi. "We'll find you a library. I'll come with you to the door, but since you're the main character, you'll have to do the rest."

Three old men sitting behind a counter looked up as Henry entered the building. Henry had found the library at last!

"Hello," said Henry. "Do you have—"

WILLIAM SHAKESPEARE (scratching his nose): "To have or not to have, that is the question. This is but a small library, but if there's one thing we do have aplenty, 'tis books."

"Do you have *The Story of the Search for the Story?*" asked Henry. "The copy my uncle has in his bathroom is nothing but blank pages and loose letters."

HENRIK IBSEN (looking suspiciously at Henry): "What is lost to God is gain."

"These two make a drama out of everything," said the man in armor. "I think I'll step in here. I'm Miguel de Cervantes. Blank pages and loose letters, you say? It sounds like the censors have been at work again."

"The censors?" asked Henry.

"The censors have always ruined books," said Cervantes. "They go in for jingle-juggling, fable-fitting, tale-tinkering, and suchlike. Was your book a classic? Let's go see if we can find another copy."

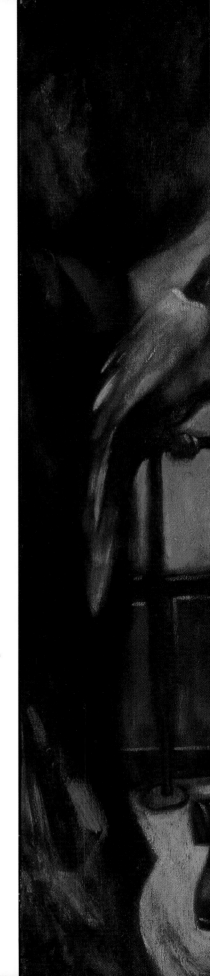

"Here we have every story imaginable—and many that are impossible to imagine," said Cervantes. "It's a shame that the censors ruin some of them."

"Why do they ruin books?" asked Henry.

"They're afraid of books they don't understand," Cervantes explained. "And they're afraid of ideas that are new and different from their own. There are plenty of those in good books. But here, the books are in alphabetical order. You can look through the shelves. Good luck!"

There wasn't a ladder, so Henry had to climb up the shelves. Higher and higher he climbed, until he finally found books that began with *S. Sa . . . Sc . . . Se . . .* Henry searched until he came to *St.* There it was—*The Story of the Search for the Story!*

But just as Henry pulled the book from the shelf, he felt a huge, cold shadow behind him. Suddenly, everything disappeared and Henry was falling, falling, falling . . .

. . . into emptiness. What had happened? Where were all the books? It was as if the whole room—the whole world—had just turned white and empty. Henry saw nothing but a few loose letters lying around.

Henry shut his eyes and opened them again, but nothing changed. He pinched himself to see if he was still there. Then a paper airplane came sailing through the air. Henry reached up and caught it. He unfolded the paper and read:

Dear main character in the stylish cap, What we feared most has happened. The censors have tried to end this story. It's dreadful to be nowhere, but don't be afraid. Just follow the few remaining letters.

S. B. and others

Henry followed the scattered letters on and on. At last colors began to appear again. Then he saw an enormous, dark shape in front of him. It was a huge building. A man stood in the shadows by a door. Henry could feel his heart pounding, but he went up to the man anyway.

"Are you the censor in this story?" asked Henry, his voice just shaking a little.

"No, no, no! That's that last thing I am. I'm Franz Kafka. I'm just standing here guarding my castle, a rather hopeless task."

Henry's heart beat more calmly. "What's inside your castle?" he asked.

"Well, lots of people have wondered about that. And many think they know. But they don't realize that the important thing is not to understand, but to marvel. The people who think they know the most actually want to close up my castle and stop me, the author, from ever creating another one."

"Can I go inside?" Henry asked.

Kafka stood up straight. "I must forbid you entry to the castle in the strongest terms," he said. Then he looked at Henry with dark eyes. "But now that I've said that, I can tell you that I like main characters who think for themselves."

Henry thought for a moment. Then he went through the door and into the darkness.

At first, Henry couldn't make out anything. Then he saw a man with a cautious smile on his face.

"So you're here at last," said the man. "With your stylish cap and all. We'd almost given up hope. You've done a good job so far—with a little help from us."

"So it was you who sent all the paper airplanes," said Henry. "You must be . . ."

"I suppose you could say I represent the Shah of Blah. I created him in a story, after all. I'm Salman Rushdie. There are hundreds of other authors here, too.

"Why are you sitting here in the dark?" asked Henry.

"We're prisoners," explained Rushdie. "We were put in here because of the stories we wrote. There seems to be more and more of us every day. We were afraid the outside world would forget us and no one would miss our stories. That's why we sent out the paper airplanes. We needed to find someone like you."

"But how can I help?" asked Henry.

"You can let people know we are here and that we long to tell our stories. If you don't, the very worst will happen."

"What is the very worst?" Henry asked anxiously.

"The very worst that could happen is that people would lose the freedom to think and write what they want. The world would lose its color. Princesses, for example, would no longer be saved by princes. Love would disappear, and life would become so dull and gray that it would be unbearable. We would lose everything, just like you did in the library."

Rushdie sighed heavily. "That's why people need stories."

"I see," said Henry. "But what will happen to me now? How does this story end?"

Rushdie handed Henry a book. "Here you are. *The Story of the Search for the Story* is your tale. Now you must tell it to someone. That's the whole point of stories. Come with me, up to the highest turret, and we'll arrange your journey home."

Rushdie and all the other authors started up the stairs. They climbed and climbed, and then they climbed some more. As Henry panted up after them, he began to feel like someone was following him. Faster and faster he climbed.

At the very top of the stairs was a tiny window. It was just big enough for Henry to sit on the sill.

"Here," said Rushdie. "Take hold of these strings. Are you ready?"

Henry looked down and felt his stomach turn over. "Ready for what?"

"For this, of course," said Rushdie, and he gave Henry a gentle push.

Henry found himself back in Uncle Richard's bathroom. The green cap was gone. He must have lost it during the flight. Henry's uncle had filled the bathtub and was about to get in.

"You've been away a long time, lad," said Uncle Richard. "What happened to you? Did they have the book at the library?"

"No," said Henry, "I kind of had to write the book myself. I got home by an awfully roundabout way, but that's often how it is in books."

Henry held out the book he was carrying and smiled. "I think we should trade places today, Uncle. Here—you do the reading."

"But—" said Uncle Richard.

"I think you'll be quite surprised by the main character and all the things he's been through," said Henry as he took off his clothes and sank down into the hot water.

Uncle Richard sat down on a pile of books, cleared his throat, and began to read:

Once upon a time, there was a boy named Henry who was very fond of books. Each evening, his uncle would read him a story . . .

Here are all the authors and characters from world literature that Henry met:

James Joyce (1882–1941)
was an Irish author who wrote novels, short stories, and poetry. He is probably most famous for his great novel *Ulysses* (1922). The novel describes the events of one day in the city of Dublin. That day is June 16, 1904—the same day that Joyce met Nora, his future wife. In *Ulysses*, Joyce used many different writing styles, including an unusual style called "stream-of-consciousness," in which he expressed the thoughts running through the minds of his characters. At first no one wanted to publish Joyce's strange new novel. But eventually, *Ulysses* was recognized as one of the greatest books ever written.

Knut Hamsun (1859–1952)
was a Norwegian writer who won the Nobel Prize for Literature in 1920. Hamsun was one of the first people to write about the things that take place in our imagination, thoughts, and dreams. He called this "the unconscious life of the mind." During World War II, he supported Hitler and the Nazis, and since then people have had a hard time accepting his work. But over the years, both writers and readers have returned to his books. The yellow suit and the two green feathers he wears in this story are borrowed from his novels *Mysteries* (1892) and *Pan* (1894).

Virginia Woolf (1882–1941)
was an English writer who had something in common with James Joyce, because she also used stream-of-consciousness techniques. Woolf felt that everyone's life was made up of thousands of tiny moments. Many of her books are about the exact colors, sounds, and feelings that people experience during these moments. Her books are very popular with readers all over the world. Henry meets Virginia Woolf while she's writing the novel *To the Lighthouse* (1927).

Ernest Hemingway (1899–1961)
grew up in the United States but lived in many different countries. He spent World War I in Italy as an ambulance driver and journalist. Later, he traveled to places such as France, Spain, and Cuba. He based the plots for many of his novels and short stories on the experiences he had in these countries. When Henry meets Hemingway, he is writing one of his greatest books, *The Old Man and the Sea* (1952).

Karen Blixen/Isak Dinesen (1885–1962)
was born in Denmark but moved to Africa after she married her cousin, Baron Bror Blixen. In Kenya she ran a coffee plantation, hunted wild animals, and wrote. "There are two pieces of advice I'd give to all young

women" she once said, "cut your hair short, and learn to drive a motor-car." After she returned to Denmark, she wrote her book *Out of Africa* (1937), which weaves together stories based on her life in Kenya. "The sublime art is, and will remain, the story. In the beginning was the story," she wrote in her book *Last Tales* (1957.)

Antoine de Saint-Exupéry (1900–1944) was a French pilot and writer. Many of his books are about his adventures as an aviator. Saint-Exupéry often wrote about the responsibilities we have as human beings. One of his most popular books, *The Little Prince* (1943), tells the story of a pilot who meets a mysterious and wise little visitor from Asteroid B-612. During World War II, Saint-Exupéry took off on a flight from which he never returned. Perhaps he flew off to look for the Little Prince one last time?

Marcel Proust (1871–1922) was one of France's greatest novelists. He spent most of his adult life writing a huge novel called *Remembrance of Things Past* (1913–27/1922–31). His novel was more than 3,300 pages long by the time he died. Proust based his book on his own lifetime of memories. He describes these memories in such great detail that he seems to make time stand still. Madeleines and tea are very important to Proust. The main character in *Remembrance of Things Past* suddenly recalls his childhood memories after one taste of a madeleine dipped in tea.

Astrid Lindgren (1907–) is a children's author from Sweden. She introduced readers around the world to characters such as Pippi Longstocking— the strongest girl in the world. Pippi had her own problems with censors when some of them tried to edit the books about her. They wanted to make Pippi more like the kind of girl they thought she should be. Luckily, Astrid Lindgren managed to stop them. In this book, the red-haired Pippi helps Henry find what he's searching for.

William Shakespeare (1564–1616) is perhaps the most famous poet and playwright the world has ever known. He lived in England hundreds of years ago, but his work continues to entertain and fascinate us. Shakespeare wrote powerful plays about tragedy and comedy—the sad and joyful sides of life. His plays are full of proud kings, evil villains, and young lovers. They are also filled with language that he invented. Because of Shakespeare, we have words like *lonely, hurry,* and *bump,* and expressions like "catch cold" and "dead as a doornail." It's in the play *Hamlet* (1600–01) that the main character speaks the famous line: "To be or not to be: that is the question."

Henrik Ibsen (1828–1906) was a Norwegian playwright. His plays, which are performed in theaters all over the world, can be deeply serious or playfully amusing. "What is lost to God is gain. For the victory is to lose all!" says the strong-willed priest in the play *Brand* (1866). On the other hand, *Peer Gynt* (1867) is about an irresponsible man. Peer betrays his great love, but she remains faithful to him. Ibsen's plays changed the way people thought about drama throughout the world.

Miguel Cervantes (1547–1616)

was a Spanish writer who published the famous novel *Don Quixote* (1605/1615). It's about a man who believes that he is a knight named Don Quixote. He fights injustice in a pretend world where windmills are giants, flocks of sheep are armies, and peasant girls are princesses. His faithful attendant, Sancho Panza, is more practical and down to earth. Together they form one of the most well-known duos in world literature. Cervantes's novel has amused readers for hundred of years.

Franz Kafka (1883–1924)

was a German Jew who lived in what later became the Czech Republic. His most well-known novels are probably *The Trial* (1925) and *The Castle* (1926). A friend published them after Kafka died, even though Kafka didn't want them printed at all. Many readers of Kafka's stories and novels have puzzled about what exactly he was trying to say. Perhaps Kafka's message was a secret he wanted to share with just a select group of readers.

Salman Rushdie (1947–)

is a British citizen who was born in India and has lived in both the East and the West. Readers around the world enjoy his imaginative books, which have won many awards. His book for children, *Haroun and the Sea of Stories* (1990), is the tale of a boy about Henry's age. Haroun must help his father, the Shah of Blah, regain his talent for storytelling. Rushdie is no stranger to the censors. His life was threatened because of a book he wrote called *The Satanic Verses* (1988).

Hundreds of other authors

have been persecuted, sentenced to death, put in prison, or have had to flee their homelands because of things they have written. Unfortunately, there isn't space in this book to tell of them all. But there is an organization called International P.E.N. (poets, playwrights, editors, essayists, and novelists) that keeps track of these writers and works to help them regain their freedom.

Henry

A boy of nine who—although he doesn't quite realize it—is the main character in his own book, *The Story of the Search for the Story*. He has a slightly younger sister named Anna, who is the main character in a book called *Anna's Art Adventure*.

First American edition published in 2000 by Carolrhoda Books, Inc.
Translated by James Anderson

Pippi Longstocking appears by permission of the Kerstin Kvint Agency AB
and with the acknowledgment of Viking Children's Publishing, a division of
Penguin Putnam Inc.

The Shah of Blah appears by permission of Salman Rushdie and
the Wylie Agency.

Carolrhoda Books, Inc.
A Division of Lerner Publishing Group
241 First Avenue North, Minneapolis, MN 55401 U.S.A.

Website address: www.lernerbooks.com

Library of Congress Cataloging-in-Publication Data

Sortland, Bjorn, 1968-
    [Forteljinga om Jakta pa Forteljinga. English]
    The story of the search for the story / written by Bjorn Sortland ;
illustrated by Lars Elling.
        p.   cm.
    Summary: Henry sets off to find a book to read to his uncle
and ends up creating his own story.
        ISBN 1-57505-375-6 (alk. paper)
    [1. Books and reading—Fiction 2. Characters in literature—Fiction.]
I. Elling, Lars, ill. II. Title.
    PZ7.S218St 1999
    [Fic]—dc21   98-46967

Manufactured in the United States of America
1 2 3 4 5 6 – 05 04 03 02 01 00